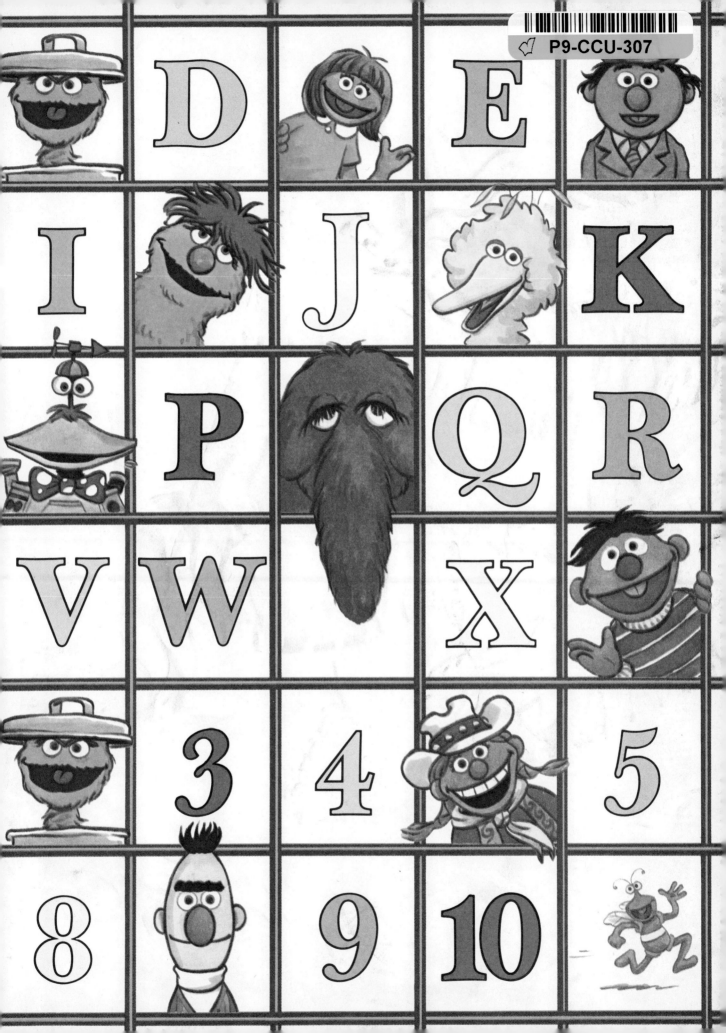

THE SESAME STREET
TREASURY

Featuring Jim Henson's Sesame Street Muppets

VOLUME 1

STARRING
THE NUMBER
1
AND THE LETTER
A

Children's Television Workshop / Funk & Wagnalls, Inc.

WRITTEN BY:

Linda Bove with
the National Theatre of the Deaf
Michael Frith
Emily Perl Kingsley
Sharon Lerner
Jeffrey Moss
Norman Stiles
Ellen Weiss
Daniel Wilcox

ILLUSTRATED BY:

Tom Cooke
A. Delaney
Mary Grace Eubank
Michael Frith
Randy Jones
Joe Mathieu
Maggie Swanson

PHOTOGRAPHS BY:

Neil Selkirk
View-Master International Group

ISBN: 0-8343-0052-4 (set); 0-8343-0053-2 (vol. 1)
1 2 3 4 5 6 7 8 9 0

One for Big Bird

It was Big Bird's birthday, and all of Sesame Street was helping him celebrate. There were birdseed cakes, games, songs, and jellybeans for everyone.

"What a great party," said the birthday bird. "This cake is so good that I think I'll just have another piece."

"Go ahead," said Betty Lou. "You have just one birthday a year. Today you're number one."

"That gives me a terrific idea," said the Count. "We can play a counting game."

Everybody sighed.

"Don't worry," said the Count. "We will only count to one."

"What kind of a game is that?" asked Big Bird.

"A *wonderful* game, of course!" cried the Count. "I will start. Do you see the sun, up there in the sky?"

Everyone looked up. Sure enough, there was the sun, hanging in its usual place.

"Now I will count," said the Count, taking a deep breath. "One!" he said happily. "One sun."

"So, how do we play the game?" asked Ernie.

"You must name something that is one of a kind," said the Count. "The only one in the world!"

"Okay," said Ernie. "There's one sun, and there's one moon too. Only one moon in the whole, wide world."

The Count clapped his hands in delight. "One. One moon!"

"I have something that there's only one of!" announced Bert.

"What could that be, old buddy?" asked Ernie. "What could you possibly have that isn't matched anywhere in the world?"

"You know, Ernie," said Bert, looking insulted. "She lives on the roof of 123 Sesame Street."

Everyone looked puzzled.

"In all the world," said Bert, "there is only one pigeon as great as Bernice." Bert was bursting with pride as he presented his pet pigeon. "Bernice, do your trick!" he commanded. "One. One Bernice!" said Bert as Bernice rolled over.

"That was wonderful," said the Count. "Now it is time for Betty Lou to think of something."

Betty Lou thought and thought. "This is not very easy," she said.

"I'm sure you can do it," said the Count. "All you need is one thing. Ha, ha, ha."

"Wait a minute!" said Betty Lou. "I know there is only one Sesame Street. It's where we live."

"Right!" said the Count, applauding gleefully.

The Count turned to Big Bird. "And now," he said, "it is your turn."

"Gee," said Big Bird. "You've all said such good things. I just can't think of a thing that is so special that there's only one in the whole world. I guess I'm not very good at this."

Big Bird looked down at his feet in embarrassment. As he stood there staring at his feet, something strange happened. He began to wiggle his toes. Then he began to smile. "I know!" he cried. "Look at my feet. There's nobody who has feet just like mine. And nobody with the same long legs. What about *all* of me? There is *only one me*!"

"One Big Bird!" cried the Count. "Wonderful."

"There isn't anybody just like me, is there?" asked Big Bird.

"No, Big Bird," said Betty Lou. "There isn't anybody like you in the whole world." And she gave him a great big birthday hug.

When Is It Spring?

When raindrops have a tune to play,
When the grass gets greener every day,
When flowers blossom everywhere,
When there's something magic in the air,

When a winding road calls to our feet,
When we just can't stay on Sesame Street,
When we hear some baby robins sing,
We're absolutely sure it's spring!

Cookie Monster's Famous Cookie Dough

Dear Reader,

Hello, there! Me COOKIE MONSTER and my favorite thing is EATING COOKIES.

In this wonderful set of books me going to show you how to make ALL KINDS OF COOKIES! But first... me tell you secret recipe for

COOKIE DOUGH (It been in my family for years.)

Here is what you need:

A medium-sized mixing bowl
Measuring cup and spoons
A fork

Butter or margarine (soft, but not melted)

Sugar
2 eggs
Vanilla

All-purpose flour
Baking powder
Salt

What to do to make the dough:

1. Put ¾ cup of butter or margarine (that's a stick and a half) into your mixing bowl.

2. Measure 1 cup of sugar.

3. Pour sugar over butter.

4. With a fork, squash butter and sugar together until they are blended.

5. Crack shells of 2 eggs and pour eggs over mixture in bowl.

6. Measure 1 tea-spoon vanilla and pour over mixture.

7. With fork, blend everything in the bowl together.

8. Measure 2½ cups of all-purpose flour and pour over mixture in bowl.

9. Measure 1 teaspoon baking powder and sprinkle over flour.

10. Measure 1 teaspoon salt and sprinkle over flour and baking powder.

11. Mix everything together either with the fork or with your hands.

12. Put dough in icebox to chill (at least one hour).

You can make LOTS of dough at once and keep it in your icebox in a plastic bag (it will last a long time). Then whenever you make COOKIES, just take out as much as you need.

In the Sesame Street Treasury me tell you how to use this yummy dough to make yummy COOKIES.

Love,

Cookie

Big Bird

Home:	The Nest, Sesame Street
Favorite Foods:	Birdseed soup, peanut butter and birdseed sandwiches, birdseed ice cream
Favorite Drink:	Birdseed float
Best Friend:	Mr. Snuffle-upagus
Pet:	Barkley
Favorite Activities:	Roller skating, hopscotch, and hide-and-seek
Height:	8 feet 2 inches
Favorite Color:	Yellow
Favorite Wish:	To introduce Mr. Snuffle-upagus to Sesame Street friends
Favorite Saying:	"Everyone makes mistakes, so why can't I?"

Help Little Red Riding Hood find the right path to Granny's birthday party.

a A

An **A** Story

Once upon a time, in a far-away kingdom, there lived a queen named Queen Agatha. One day, Queen Agatha called all the knights of the kingdom to the throne room.

I love things that begin with **A**!

"Knights of the kingdom," announced Queen Agatha, "I love things that begin with A. Whoever can bring me something that begins with the letter A will be rewarded handsomely. *Perhaps* the winner will dance with me at the royal party tonight."

"Oh, boy!" said Sir Bird. "I'm heading for the Royal Zoo! That's the only place where I can find something that begins with the letter A. I'll be right back, Queen Agatha!"

Sir Bird hurried from the throne room, pausing only long enough to take an apple from a bowl near the throne room door.

"I'd better bring this apple with me," he said, "in case I get hungry on my way to the zoo."

Once outside the castle, Sir Bird realized that he was lost.

"Oh, no, I'm lost!" cried Sir Bird. "If only there were something to help me find my way to the Royal Zoo."

Just then, Sir Bird passed a large arrow. The arrow said, "This way to the zoo."

"Oh, look at that arrow!" exclaimed Sir Bird. "That arrow will help me find my way."

So he grabbed the arrow and followed it until he reached his destination—a cage in the Royal Zoo where there sat a happy-looking alligator.

"Oh, Mr. Alligator, I've found you at last," said Sir Bird. "Your name begins with the letter A. Won't you please come with me, back to the throne room?"

Since the alligator had never before seen a throne room, he was more than happy to follow Sir Bird.

When he reached the throne room,
Sir Bird announced to the Queen,
"Queen Agatha, this alligator's name
begins with the letter A. I guess
now I can dance with you
at the royal party,
huh?"

"Well," said the Queen,
"first of all that apple and that arrow
you have also begin with the letter A."

"Oh, how silly of me!" said Sir Bird. "I grabbed the apple
and the arrow without realizing that they began with
the letter A. But I guess that since I brought you an apple
and an arrow and an alligator, I can dance with you at the
royal party for sure."

"Well…if it's all the same to you, I'd like to dance with your friend! You're a pretty handsome guy, you know that?" said the Queen to the alligator.

Then she said to Sir Bird, "Sir Bird, since you found the letter A, I will give you a lifetime supply of birdseed. And, I will make you my Ambassador to Antarctica."

"Oh, boy!" said Sir Bird. And Sir Bird was very happy. And so was the Queen. As for the alligator, he was happy, too, because he had always wanted to dance with a Queen. And since everybody is happy, the story is over.

ANIMALES   ANIMALS

Say it in Spanish!

granja
farm

gallo
rooster

perro
dog

maggie

vaca
cow

caballo
horse

gato
cat

cerdo
pig

oveja
sheep

ganso
goose

cabra
goat

gallina
hen

"Do you know what this is, Little Bird?"

"Sure, Big Bird. It's a stick!"

"Not what I'm pointing *with*, Little Bird. What am I pointing *at*?"

"Oh . . . hmm . . . let's see . . ."

"It's the alphabet, Little Bird. Just think—every word you can think of is made from these letters!"

"Even 'stick'?"

"Yes, Little Bird. Even 'stick.'"

Good

morning

In the Morning

alarm clock

bed

window

sunrise

toothpaste

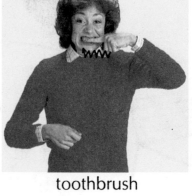

toothbrush

wake up

comb

cup

mirror

Good morning!

It's time

to get up.

Grover's Bedtime Story

"Thank you very much for inviting me to sleep over at your house, Grover," said Prairie Dawn. "I've had such a good time."

"Oh, it is fun to have somebody come to visit and sleep over," said Grover. "I am glad you could come. But now it is late and I think we had better go to sleep."

"Uh, Grover?" said Prairie Dawn.

"There is just one little thing. I like to hear a bedtime story before I go to sleep. When I am home, my daddy usually tells me a story."

"Hmm. That is a problem," said Grover. "We could call your daddy on the telephone and he could tell you a story over the phone. How would that be?"

"I have a better idea," said Prairie

Dawn. "Why don't *you* tell me a bedtime story?"

"Me?" said Grover. "*Me??* Cute, furry, adorable old Grover? Tell you a bedtime story?"

"Why not?" said Prairie Dawn. "I am sure you know lots of nice stories."

"Er, well," said Grover, "I have not told many bedtime stories before. In fact, *none* is how many bedtime stories I have told. None at all. I really do not know how to tell a bedtime story."

"Oh, I am sure you can do it," said Prairie Dawn. "You just start at the beginning and the rest will take care of itself." She got into bed and pulled the covers up around her chin. "O.K., Grover, I am ready. You can start your bedtime story now."

"Oh, dear," said Grover. "How to do this. . . . Just start at the beginning and see what happens, huh? Ahem. All right. . . .

"Once upon a time . . ." he began. "Yes, that is an excellent *beginning* to my story. Once upon a time! Once upon a time. Once upon a time."

"Uh, Grover," said Prairie Dawn, "what comes next?"

"I beg your pardon?" asked Grover.

"Well," said Prairie Dawn, "all you said was 'Once upon a time.' There has to be more to the story than that! That is just a *beginning* to the story. What happens next?"

"Ohhhh," said Grover. "You want to know what happens next! Of course you do! Heh, heh. Um . . . well . . . let me see. . . .

"Once upon a time," Grover began again, ". . . um . . . well . . . they lived happily ever after! There you are!"

"Grover!" said Prairie Dawn. "What kind of story is that? That is not the way to tell a story! Once upon a time they lived happily ever after? That is ridiculous!"

"You did not like the way it ended?" asked Grover. "I always thought 'they lived happily ever after' was a very nice ending to a story."

"The beginning was O.K., and the ending was O.K. . . . but there was no middle."

"No middle?" said Grover. "What is a *middle*?"

"The middle is the *story* part of the story—where everything happens!" explained Prairie Dawn. "You left out the whole middle part!"

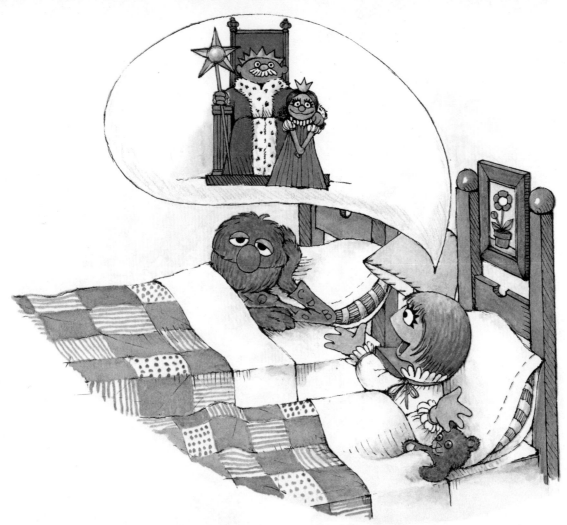

"I am sorry, Prairie Dawn," said Grover. "I told you I did not have much experience in telling bedtime stories."

"Well, let me show you how it works," said Prairie Dawn. "Then you will know how, and you can tell me *my* bedtime story."

"That is an excellent idea!" said Grover.

"O.K.," said Prairie Dawn. "First you start your story with 'Once upon a time,' just as you did. But then you follow it with the middle part of the story. So here goes:

"Once upon a time there was a king named Roundtree and he had a very smart and beautiful daughter named Victoria Joyce. One day a wicked magician came and put a spell on the three good fairies who were weaving an enchanted cloak in

which to wrap the mysterious silver apple so that it could be delivered to the wondrous wizard of the West, so their fingers turned into string beans and they could no longer weave the enchanted cloak. But the brave little girl mesmerized the six fire-breathing dragons that guarded the castle gate and flew on the magic flying horse, Basingstoke, through the skies, dodging the evil eagles and horrid hawks that swooped and darted at her, on to the wizard's palace, where she delivered the silver apple to the wizard all by herself. The wizard was so amazed at Victoria's splendid feats of bravery and courage that he presented her with a beautiful singing bird and a flower that would always be in bloom. The evil witches on the mountains gnashed their

teeth and pulled out their hair
because they had wanted the
singing bird and the amazing ever-
blooming flower but they knew they
could not fight against such a
glorious girl as Victoria Joyce and
Victoria sailed home to her father's
castle on the back of a great golden
swan ... and ... and here is where
you put the ending part on, Grover,
and ... she lived happily ever after!

"There. You see how easy it is
to tell a bedtime story? But you
absolutely must have the middle
part or else it is not a story at
all. Do you understand now,
Grover? ... Grover? ... Grover??"

But Grover had fallen fast asleep.

"Oh dear," said Prairie Dawn.
"Now I've *done* it. I told such a good
story that I put Grover to sleep. Now
what am I going to do? I'll be up all
night."

Just then the door opened and
Grover's mommy came into the
room.

"Would you like to hear a bedtime
story, Prairie Dawn?" asked Grover's
mommy. "I used to tell bedtime
stories to Grover but he would
always fall asleep right after the
'Once upon a time' part. He never
heard the middle and the end. It
would be a great treat for me to be
able to tell a bedtime story to
someone who could stay awake long
enough to hear the 'happily ever
after' part."

"Oh, thank you," said Prairie
Dawn. And she curled up under the
covers as Grover's mommy sat down
beside the bed.

"Once upon a time ..." began
Grover's mommy. ...

Big Bird's COLORS

GREEN is the color of Granny Bird's couch,
of grass and of spinach and Oscar the Grouch.

It's not easy being green.

Cookie and Grover and Herry are **BLUE**,
and bluebirds and bluebells
and blueberries, too.

Do you prefer the gold or silver trim?

This flower is **PURPLE** and so are these grapes,
and so are ALL of Prince Charming's fine capes.

RED is tomatoes, stoplights and cherries,
and strawberry jam— and that necktie of Herry's!

An orange is **ORANGE**
and so is Bert's nose—
and Ernie is orange—and so are my toes.

YELLOW bananas—and a big bumblebee,
and daisies and butter
—and don't forget ME!

Find the Things That Begin with the Letter **A**

The Count's Counting Page

Greetings! It is I, the Count!
In **1** moment, I will eat my delicious lunch.
But first, I will count the things in my lunch.
Here is a sandwich.
That's **1** scrumptious sandwich. Ha, ha, ha!
Here is a carrot.
That's **1** lovely carrot.
Here is a carton of milk.
That's **1** wonderful carton of milk.
And here . . . Wait just **1** minute!
I thought I had **1** tasty oatmeal cookie.
Where did my **1** cookie go?
Ah, well, I still have **1** marvelous lunch! Ha, ha, ha!

Good Night, Rubber Duckie

"It's getting late, Ernie," said Bert, "and my whole family of sisters and brothers and aunts and uncles and cousins are coming to visit us first thing in the morning." Bert snuggled down into his warm, cozy bed. "Why don't you finish what you're doing and get into bed?"

"I'm almost finished, Bert, old pal," said Ernie, putting his toothbrush back in the holder. "I washed my face and hands and I brushed my teeth. And now I'm ready to get ready for bed."

"Ready to get ready? What do you mean?" asked Bert.

"Well, I can't jump into bed just like that," replied Ernie. "I have to make sure I have everything I need for sleeping. Now let's see. . . . First let me check and see if I have my blanket and my pillow. . . ."

"Of course you have your blanket and your pillow, Ernie," said Bert. "Your bed has the same blanket and sheets and pillow that it's always had."

"Well, that's true," said Ernie, "but you can't be too careful. I wouldn't want to get into bed and all comfy-cozy and *then* find that my pillow or my blanket wasn't there."

"All right, all right," said Bert. "Your pillow and blanket are there. Now will you *please* go to bed!"

"Just a second, Bert," said Ernie. "I have a few other things to check."

"Oh, brother," sighed Bert.

"Hmm," said Ernie, looking around. "My alarm clock is set to go off in the morning. . . . My night light is on in case I need to get up and go to the bathroom during the night. . . . My hockey stick is ready in case anybody comes and invites me to a midnight game of hockey. . . . And my Rubber Duckie . . . my Rubber Duckie is . . . my . . . OH NO!"

Joe Mathieu

"What's the matter?" asked Bert.

"My Rubber Duckie! My Rubber Duckie's not on my bed!" yelled Ernie.

"Come on, Ernie," said Bert. "Your Rubber Duckie is always right there on your bed. I'm sure it's there."

"No, no, it's not," sobbed Ernie. "How can I possibly go to sleep without my Rubber Duckie?!"

"Millions of people have been doing it for years, Ernie. Come on, go to sleep, and we'll find your Duckie in the morning."

"SLEEP WITHOUT RUBBER DUCKIE?" yelled Ernie. "What if I told you to go to sleep without your paper clips? Huh? Huh? What then?"

"That's different," said Bert.

"It is not! And I'm not going to sleep without my Rubber Duckie!" said Ernie. "And you're going to help me find him."

"Ohhhhhh no," said Bert. "What I am going to do is lie here in my nice, warm, cozy bed and go to sleep. If you want to stay up all night looking for your Rubber Duckie, go ahead. But I'm going to sleep. Good night!"

"All right, Bert," said Ernie. "Whatever you say. I'll find Rubber Duckie all by myself. YOO-HOO! RUBBER DUCKIE! RUBBER DUCKIE, WHERE ARE YOU?"

"All right, all right, I'll help you." Bert gave in. "Come on, let's find your Rubber Duckie so we can both get some sleep."

"O.K.," said Ernie. "You look in the refrigerator, and I'll look in the coat closet."

"In the refrigerator?" said Bert. "What would your Rubber Duckie be doing in the refrigerator?"

"You know how hungry he gets just before he goes to bed," said Ernie.

Bert looked in the refrigerator. There were pickles and salamis and leftover meat loaf and grapefruits and applesauce and Ernie's ice skates—but no Rubber Duckie.

Ernie checked the coat closet. There were hats and coats and jackets and galoshes and gloves and his old stuffed toy elephant—but no Rubber Duckie.

"I'm looking in the bathroom," shouted Bert. He found towels and soap and toothpaste and toilet paper and a shower curtain and a

washcloth and Ernie's cowboy hat—
but no Rubber Duckie.

"I'll check out the toybox,"
suggested Ernie. "Maybe he fell in
there after we played with our toys
tonight." Ernie found his fire engine
and his blocks and his paint set and
his Messy Bessy doll and his racing
cars and his marking pen and his
dollhouse and his dinosaur model kit
and a piece of pepperoni pizza—but
no Rubber Duckie.

"I'm checking under the beds,"
said Bert. He looked under the beds
and found some shoes and slippers
and a book and a baseball and
Ernie's R collection and Ernie's
ukelele and a package of marigold

seeds—but no Rubber Duckie.

"I'll check the laundry hamper.
Maybe he fell in there while I was
getting undressed," said Ernie.
Ernie looked in the laundry hamper
and he found socks and undershirts
and pants and sweaters and pajamas
and underpants and his fishing rod
and his basketball—but no Rubber
Duckie.

"I give up," said Ernie, exhausted.
"I've looked everywhere. I'm just
going to have to try to sleep without
Rubber Duckie. I don't know how,
but I'll try."

"That's the spirit," said Bert. "I'm
sure we'll find Rubber Duckie in the
morning."

"I certainly hope so," said Ernie, crawling sadly into bed. He pulled up the covers and put his head down on the pillow with a sigh. Just then there was a great, big, loud SQUEAK!

"Rubber Duckie!" cried Ernie. "You were there all the time, under my pillow. Oh, Rubber Duckie! I'm so happy to find you!"

"*Now* will you go to sleep, Ernie?" asked Bert.

"Sure, Bert," said Ernie. "What in the world are you doing up so late? Don't you remember? Your whole family of brothers and sisters and aunts and uncles and cousins are coming to visit us first thing in the morning! We don't want to be all tired and baggy-eyed! Why don't you go to sleep? Good night, Bert. And good night, Rubber Duckie."

Jack be nimble, Jack be quick,
Jack jump over the candlestick.